Dedicated to Kamilla for planting a seed,
and to Aniko for always encouraging the bloom

Winnie & Waldorf: Disobedience School
Copyright © 2016 by Kati Hites
ISBN 978-0-06-231162-7

The artist used watercolors to create the illustrations for this book.
Typography by Jeanne Hogle
16 17 18 19 20 SCP 10 9 8 7 6 5 4 3 2 1
❖
First Edition

Winnie & Waldorf

Dis^Obedience School

Written and illustrated by Kati Hites

HARPER

An Imprint of HarperCollinsPublishers

I love Waldorf more than anything, but lately he has been a very bad dog.

It seems all he does is misbehave.

He even chased a pigeon right through
a big crowd, knocking people over!
That was the last straw.

I tell him it's time to apply to school.
The good news is, our interview
goes really well. He's been accepted
to Winnie's Disobedience School.

Winnie's

First, I show him his cubby, where he can put all his personal stuff during class.

He seems comfortable with it.

All smart dogs know their ABC's,
so that's our first lesson. Waldorf
catches on quickly . . .

. . . but his reading level is still pretty average.
The classics will have to wait.

Every decent, cultured dog takes music classes. Waldorf is no exception. He is a talented baritone.

Schools always have nap time.
Naturally Waldorf excels at that.

He's impressive.

How good is he in math class?
Subtraction is easy for him,

addition needs some work,

but he is simply a genius in art!

Things are going so well in his
disobedience training, until . . .

. . . his wild side comes out in gym class!

Why is Waldorf running away?
I thought he was having so much
fun in school!

Then things go terribly wrong. We realize
our neighbor's dog is loose and seems
to be heading straight for the street!

Oh no!

Watch out!

Waldorf instantly knows what to do.
No dog can resist playing fetch.

He passes the tennis ball. . . .

And the little dog catches it . . . instead of running into the street!

Waldorf saves him!

He is so heroic. Especially
when he is just being himself.

To celebrate, I teach Waldorf
my favorite dance move.

'Round and around we go!

We pirouette straight into Mom!

She tells me to get ready for bed. It's been a long and busy day, and tomorrow will be time for ME to go to school!

Before bedtime, we have to clean up all our classroom equipment.

It gives us a chance to go over everything we learned.

It's a good thing Waldorf behaved
so well in my school because . . .

. . . I think he's ready to walk me all the way to kindergarten without any mishaps.

322 4249